THE BLUNDER OF THE ROGUES

written and illustrated by **Tim Egan**

Houghton Mifflin Company   Boston 1999

For Sue, Steve, Cuyler, Sally, Tim, Andy and Sadie.

www.houghtonmifflinbooks.com

Library of Congress Cataloging-in-Publication Data

Egan, Tim.
The blunder of the rogues / written and illustrated by Tim Egan.
p.   cm.
Summary: The Rogues, a band of mischievous young animals,
are transformed into real crooks when they get involved with
Vincent the goat and an innocent-looking little old sheep lady.
RNF ISBN 0-395-91007-2 PAP ISBN 0-618-25075-1
[1. Criminals—Fiction. 2. Animals—Fiction.] I. Title.
PZ7.E2815Bl   1999
[Fic]—DC21   98-10185   CIP AC

Manufactured in the United States of America
BVG 10 9 8 7 6 5 4 3 2

The night we were first arrested, it was so cold that our fingers hurt. We were writing on the wall behind the Klondike Theatre when the white lights caught us from behind.

"Freeze!" came the command from the squad car.

"We're already freezing!" I yelled back, to the amusement of my fellow delinquents. The police didn't laugh. We spent the night in jail.

My name is Skunk. I'm actually a raccoon, but I guess I didn't bathe enough when I was younger and the nickname stuck.

Mick, the gorilla, wasn't really very tough, but he always kept a toothpick in his mouth, which somehow made him look tougher. I'm still not sure why that is.

Sneaky, the rat, was just that . . . sneaky. I'm not saying that he was a cheater, but you definitely didn't want to play cards with this guy.

Jake, the walrus, was, and still is, my best friend. He wore an eye patch for a while because, like Mick's toothpick, he thought it made him look tough. But he got a rash from it so he had to take it off.

Vincent, the goat, was the newest member of our little group, and, as we would find out later, he was also the cleverest.

We actually didn't start out as bad guys but rather as a bowling team. Our team was called the Rogues. One night, after losing again, we were walking home complaining, as always. We were rotten bowlers. We couldn't dance or sing. We weren't scientists or mechanics or lawyers or musicians or carpenters. We felt like we weren't good at anything.

Then Mick, in his frustration, kicked over a trash can, spilling garbage everywhere. For some strange reason, I laughed and said, "You big oaf, look at the mess you made." Then Sneaky laughed a little, then Jake. So Mick kicked over another one. We all laughed again. Twenty-three trash cans later we were hysterical and I had the worst idea of my life. "Hey, I know! Let's become criminals!" I said. "We're no good at anything else." Everyone agreed and it was settled.

We kept the name Rogues because we couldn't think of anything better.

That week we started doing all sorts of rotten things. Stepping on flowers. Ringing doorbells and running away. Crossing the street when the light said "Don't walk." Scaring pigeons.

We felt dangerous.

Then, one night, we decided it was time to try a really big crime. So while Sneaky, Jake and I kept a lookout, Mick stole the hubcaps off an old jalopy. Our hearts were pounding as we watched him perform the dastardly deed.

"Why are we doing this?" Jake asked nervously. "What are we going to do with the hubcaps?"

"Nothing," I said. "We're just doing it because it's a crime and we need the practice."

About twenty minutes later we were sitting on the sidewalk, discussing how bad we were.

"Now that we've stolen hubcaps, we're real live criminals," I said proudly.

"Yeah," agreed Sneaky. "We're like the Mafia."

"Oh, please," came a voice from behind us. "If you were real criminals, you'd have taken the whole car." We turned around and there he stood. The goat that would change our lives.

"The name's Vincent," he said. "I've been watching you for the last few days and I think you've got what it takes to be real crooks. But if you want to make it big, you've got to think big. That is, unless you want to remain the small-time hoods you are."

We were intrigued.

Vincent told us he was already a big-time criminal and we believed him. He said he'd show us some tricks of the trade.

"First," he said, "you've got to make your mark so that everyone will know who the bad guys are. You can't become notorious if nobody's ever heard of you."

The next evening Vincent convinced us to graffiti the back of the Klondike Theatre, which, as you know, led to our first arrest. We'd only known Vincent for one night and he had already landed us in the slammer.

He was a real criminal and we were fascinated.

About a week later, Vincent said it was time to hit it big. He said he'd been keeping his eye on a little old sheep lady who was apparently quite wealthy. He said she kept thousands of dollars in her purse. He said we should steal her purse.

"No way!" I said. "That's going too far." Sneaky, Jake, and Mick all agreed.

"Oh, sorry," said Vincent. "I thought you wanted to become real crooks. My mistake. Go back to scaring pigeons."

He started walking away when Jake said, "Wait."

"Wait for what?" asked Vincent. "Here she comes now. It's time to decide."

So we decided. Just then, the sheep lady came walking by and we all stepped out in front of her.

"Hand over the purse, Sheep Lady," I said cleverly, though to this day I wish I hadn't.

The little sheep lady turned out to be the most incredible martial arts expert I'd ever seen. Before we knew what was happening, she let out a really high-pitched scream and we were spinning and flying and landing in various places all over the sidewalk.

It wasn't what we'd expected.

"What a sorry-looking lot!" the sheep lady screamed. "How dare you attack me, a poor little sheep. Your rudeness is inexcusable! Someone should teach you some manners!"

Unfortunately, the dangerous sheep lady decided that SHE would teach us some manners. She told us to line up in single file and follow her back to her house. We were so dazed, we just did what she said. The word *strange* doesn't begin to describe the next few hours.

The little old sheep lady was off her rocker. A fruitcake. A weird and scary little ball of wool.

She had a whole closet full of fancy outfits that she made us change into. We had to comb our fur, brush our teeth and, get this, trim our nails.

She made us stand up straight and walk around with our heads held high and hold the door for her and bow and say things like "Pardon me, madam, after you."

It was humiliating.

After an entire afternoon of this, I carefully asked her, "Excuse me, Miss Sheep Lady, but why are you making us do all these things?"

"Why," she said, "I'm glad you asked. I figure if you present yourselves in proper fashion, no one will suspect you when you walk in and ROB THE THIRD STREET BANK!"

We were dumbfounded.

"We can't rob a bank," said Mick.

"Yeah," said Sneaky. "We wouldn't know how."

"True," said Vincent. "We're not prepared for that yet."

"Besides," I said, "we're just small-time crooks."

"Actually," said Jake, "we're just a bad bowling team that made a big mistake."

"Oh," said the crazy sheep, "maybe you'd rather I toss you across the room a couple of times! Huh? Is that what you want, Mr. Walrus? Is it?" The demented sheep lady was heading toward Jake when Vincent yelled.

"Wait!" he said. "Maybe we should do what she says. How difficult could it be?"

Not having much of a choice, we reluctantly agreed.

The next day, after working out the details, we headed to the bank, dressed like very sophisticated and respectable citizens. As we entered the building, I must admit, my paws were sweating. I was terrified. So were the others.

We walked up to the bank teller and handed him a note that said, "Please give us all your money and we'll leave quietly. Thank you and have a pleasant afternoon."

What was remarkable was that the teller handed us the money. We walked outside and handed it to the sheep lady the way she told us to. It was that easy.

But just then we heard that terrible word once again.

"Freeze!" yelled one of the two dozen police officers suddenly surrounding us.

"These are the crooks!" yelled the psycho sheep lady, pointing to us.

"What?!" I yelled in disbelief. "She made us do it! It was her idea! She's crazy!"

This time around, the police did laugh. "Ha ha ha. Yeah right, Skunk. The little ole sheep

lady made the big thugs rob the bank. Nice try. Now turn around and put your hands up."

Apparently, someone had tipped off the police to our bank heist. And as they led us away, that was when we realized that Vincent was the cleverest of us all. He had pretended to be just another bank customer. No one ever suspected he was even with us.

We were sentenced to seven years of hard labor in the federal penitentiary and, let me tell you, prison was no fun at all. The food was terrible, the other inmates were really mean and scary, the cell was cold and small, the bed was uncomfortable, and I was miserable every minute I was there.

Whenever I saw Jake or the other guys, we'd talk in great detail about what idiots we were, why we didn't just pick up that first garbage can and go home on that fateful night. Even though we weren't very good at it, we should have stuck with bowling.

I found myself writing a lot.

To my surprise, it was more satisfying writing on paper than on walls.

Mick stayed busy by lifting weights. Sneaky worked on his card tricks and Jake spent his time thinking of ways to improve the awful food we were served.

  Seven years is a long time to do without trees and cake and laughter and birthday parties and about five thousand other enjoyable things.

  We were released about three and a half years ago and as we left prison, we all knew that things were going to be different from then on.

I'm happy to report that today things are very different indeed.

About six months after being released, I met a gal named Sylvia. We're happily married and have two great kids. I now write a column for the *Klondike Herald.*

Jake became a master chef and opened a place called Tusk. It's the best and most exclusive restaurant in the city. You can't even get in without a reservation.

Mick became a fitness instructor and has a steady girlfriend named Ursula.

Sneaky is now a successful magician and is currently on a fourteen-city tour. He's played Las Vegas three times to sold-out crowds.

We're doing well, and occasionally, although we're still not very good at it, we all go bowling together. All except Vincent, that is.

Last I heard, he had convinced another group of small-time hoods to steal the purse from the little old sheep lady, who, it turns out, had been his partner long before we ever met him. They're both wanted by the authorities in connection with a string of bank robberies.